# The Tortoise and The Hare

## by Candice Cain

BAKER'S PLAYS

Baker's Plays
7611 Sunset Blvd.
Los Angeles, CA 90042
bakersplays.com

## NOTICE

This book is offered for sale at the price quoted only on the understanding that, if any additional copies of the whole or any part are necessary for its production, such additional copies will be purchased. The attention of all purchasers is directed to the following: this work is fully protected under the copyright laws of the United States of America, the British Commonwealth, including Canada, and all other countries of the Copyright Union. Violations of the Copyright Law are punishable by fine or imprisonment, or both. The copying or duplication of this work or any part of this work, by hand or by any process, is an infringement of the copyright and will be vigorously prosecuted.

This play may not be produced by amateurs or professionals for public or private performance without first submitting application for performing rights. Licensing fees are due on all performances whether for charity or gain, or whether admission is charged or not. Since performance of this play without the payment of the licensing fee renders anybody participating liable to severe penalties imposed by the law, anybody acting in this play should be sure, before doing so, that the licensing fee has been paid. Professional rights, reading rights, radio broadcasting, television and all mechanical rights, etc. are strictly reserved. Application for performing rights should be made directly to BAKER'S PLAYS.

No one shall commit or authorize any act or omission by which the copyright of, or the right to copyright, this play may be impaired. No one shall make any changes in this play for the purpose of production.

Publication of this play does not imply availability for performance. Both amateurs and professionals considering a production are strongly advised in their own interest to apply to Baker's Plays for written permission before starting rehearsals, advertising, or booking a theatre.

Whenever the play is produced, the author's name must be carried in all publicity, advertising and programs. Also, the following notice must appear on all printed programs, "Produced by special arrangement with Baker's Plays."

Licensing fees for THE TORTOISE AND THE HARE are based on a per performance rate and payable one week in advance of the production.

Please consult the Baker's Plays website at www.bakersplays.com or our current print catalogue for up to date licensing fee information.

THE TORTOISE AND THE HARE
ISBN 978-0-87440-739-6
#1657-B

# CHARACTERS

**FLASH THE HARE** - Cocky and over-confident. A braggart.

**SLY THE FOX** - Suave and intelligent.

**THEODORE THE TORTOISE** - Laid back and friendly. Happy to be included.

**TRIXIE THE BUNNY** - Silly and airheaded. A cheerleader.

**DIXIE THE BUNNY** - Silly and airheaded. A cheerleader.

**FLO THE BUNNY** - Smarter than the other two bunnies. Sarcastic and dry. A cheerleader.

**JACK THE RABBIT** - The bartender at The Rabbit Hole.

**BARBARA THE BEAVER** - The reporter for First Forest news. Can't pronounce the letter "R".

**ROXY THE RACCOON** - The camera operator for First Forest News.

**EDWINA THE OWL** - Very wise and mature.

**VARIOUS FOREST ANIMALS**

# MUSIC USE NOTE

*For Julienne and her turtle-like tendencies*

## Scene One

*(Curtains open to reveal a forest during the day.* **FLASH THE HARE** *struts onto the stage. He is wearing a track suit and running shoes. There is a very arrogant air about him.* **SLY THE FOX** *is seemingly sleeping against a tree, unnoticed by* **FLASH**. **FLASH** *addresses the audience.)*

**FLASH.** *(to audience)* I am the fastest animal in this forest. No one can beat me in a race! I raced against Roxy Raccoon and left her in the dust. I beat Harry Horse by a mile. I have raced against every animal in this forest, and I have always come in first place. Heck, I bet I'm the fastest animal in the whole world!

**SLY.** Actually, that's not true.

**FLASH.** Who said that?

*(***SLY*** *stands up and brushes himself off.)*

**SLY.** I did, silly.

**FLASH.** Oh, hi, Sly. I didn't see you there.

**SLY.** Well, I saw you, Flash. I heard everything that you said.

**FLASH.** So what? I am the fastest animal in this entire forest.

**SLY.** You don't know that for sure.

**FLASH.** Of course I do! I have beaten every single animal that lives in this forest in a race.

**SLY.** Not every animal. There is still one that you haven't raced.

**FLASH.** Who? I'll race them right now!

**SLY.** Theodore.

**FLASH.** Theodore?

**SLY.** Yup. Theodore.

**FLASH.** Theodore Tortoise?

**SLY.** That's right.

(**FLASH** *laughs at the suggestion.*)

**FLASH.** *(laughing)* Oh, that's a good one! Ha! Ha! Ha! Me and a tortoise race? Ha! That's rich!

(**SLY** *patiently watches and waits as* **FLASH** *laughs.* **FLASH** *notices that* **SLY** *isn't laughing and abruptly stops.*)

**FLASH.** *(in disbelief)* You're serious?

**SLY.** Absolutely.

**FLASH.** Sly, I can walk faster backwards with my feet tied together and blindfolded than Theodore can run.

**SLY.** That may be true, but you still haven't beaten him in a race. You can't call yourself the fastest animal in the forest until you do.

(**THEODORE TORTOISE** *enters through the back of the audience and slowly walks toward the stage.*)

**FLASH.** That is ridiculous! A tortoise in a race against a hare? I'm gonna embarrass him. I'm gonna pulverize him. He could have a three mile head start, and I'd still beat him to the finish line!

**SLY.** He doesn't need a head start, Flash. You didn't give any of the other animals a head start. You should race Theodore fair and square.

**FLASH.** Any race between a tortoise and a hare is not fair and square.

**SLY.** So, you forfeit?

**FLASH.** Me? Forfeit a race? And to Theodore Tortoise?!

(**THEODORE** *slowly climbs up the stage steps.*)

**THEODORE.** Did somebody say my name?

**SLY.** Hello, Theodore! We were just talking about you.

**THEODORE.** You were?

**SLY.** Flash was just saying that he is going to forfeit—

**FLASH.** *(interrupting)* Actually, Theo old chum, I was just saying that you are the only animal in this forest that I haven't raced.

**THEODORE.** Everyone knows that you would beat me in a race, Flash.

**FLASH.** You know it. I know it. Every animal that lives in this forest knows it. But Sly here thinks that you and I need to have a race.

*(**THEODORE** shrugs.)*

**THEODORE.** Okay.

**FLASH.** *(incredulous)* Okay?! You're actually going to race me?

**THEODORE.** Sure. Why not?

**FLASH.** Why not? Because I'll mortify you! I'll clobber you! You'll be eating my dust for a week! That's why!

**THEODORE.** Flash, everyone knows that I am slow. After all, I am a tortoise. But, it will be fun for me to actually be in the race rather than watching from the crowd.

**SLY.** Excellent. When shall the race be?

**THEODORE.** We can do it this evening, if you want.

**SLY.** That isn't enough time to get everyone to watch.

**FLASH.** Besides, I'm going to a party at the Rabbit Hole with Trixie, Dixie and Flo.

**THEODORE.** You have a date with three bunnies at the same time?

**FLASH.** Hey – When you're fast, you're fast.

**SLY.** Why not tomorrow morning?

**THEODORE.** That works for me.

**FLASH.** Yeah! Tomorrow morning! Eight o'clock sharp. See you at the finish line, tortoise!

*(**FLASH** runs off stage right. **SLY** and **THEODORE** watch after him.)*

**THEODORE.** He's going to beat me, isn't he?

**SLY.** Probably, but don't give up. You never know what may happen.

**THEODORE.** You aren't going to cheat, are you?

**SLY.** No, of course not. Flash is just a little too sure of himself. All you need to remember is that slow and steady wins the race.

**THEODORE.** Well, that's me: slow and steady.

**SLY.** See you in the morning, Theo.

**THEODORE.** Have a good day, Sly.

> *(**SLY** exits stage right as **THEODORE** slowly exits stage left. Curtains close as **THEODORE** makes his way across the stage.)*

## Scene Two

*(FLASH enters with three female bunnies. These bunnies are TRIXIE, DIXIE, and FLO. All are dressed up for a party.)*

**TRIXIE.** So, you're really going to race a turtle tomorrow?

**FLASH.** Actually, he's a tortoise.

**DIXIE.** Tortoise, turtle, they're both slower than molasses. Why bother racing if everyone knows you're going to win?

**FLASH.** That's what I said! But, if I want to be the official "Fastest Animal in the Forest," then I have to beat him in a race.

**FLO.** Are you going to do anything to prepare for it?

**FLASH.** Prepare for what?

**FLO.** The race! It is tomorrow morning, isn't it?

*(FLASH laughs. TRIXIE and DIXIE giggle along with him.)*

**FLASH.** *(sighing)* Flo, Flo, Flo. I am undeniably, unequivocally and absolutely the fastest animal in this forest. I have outrun horses and foxes. I have beaten wolves and dogs. I am even faster than any other hare that lives in these woods. No rabbit, no hare, no bunny could even come close to my speed.

**FLO.** Well, shouldn't you at least get a good night's sleep?

**TRIXIE.** Oh, wake up, Flo! Flash is the greatest!

**DIXIE.** Yeah! Why, Flash doesn't need any sleep at all!

**FLASH.** *(enjoying the praise)* Trixie, Dixie, please. You're embarrassing me.

*(SLY enters stage left. He sees FLASH and the bunnies. He steps into the shadows and listens.)*

**TRIXIE.** Hey, I got an idea! Let's make tonight a Pre-Victory Party for Flash!

**DIXIE.** Great idea, Trixie! Then tomorrow night can be the Victory Party.

**TRIXIE.** And the next night can be the Post-Victory Party.

**DIXIE.** You know what that means!

**TRIXIE & DIXIE.** *(excited)* Three nights of parties!

**FLO.** Now, wait just one minute, you two. You don't know that Flash is going to win the race.

**TRIXIE & DIXIE.** Yes we do.

**FLASH.** Flo, sweetheart, honey, baby, carrot stick, there is absolutely no way that I am going to lose this race. And if I do, I'll eat that pretty little hat of yours.

**FLO.** *(still unsure)* Well, if you are that certain that you're going to win...

**FLASH.** Believe me, I am going to win.

**FLO.** Then, I guess it's okay.

> *(***TRIXIE*** *and* ***DIXIE*** *squeal and clap their hands. The four of them face upstage in front of the center curtain closure, making sure that the audience sees their cotton tails.)*

## Scene Three

*(Curtains open to reveal the interior of The Rabbit Hole, the Forest's Night Club. Among the animals there are the bartender JACK RABBIT and the local newscaster BARBARA BEAVER. ROXY RACCOON is the camera operator for BARBARA. [NOTE: BARBARA BEAVER is the animal version of Barbara Walters. She pronounces her "l"s and "r"s as "w"s.] Other animals are dancing and having a good time. FLASH, TRIXIE, DIXIE and FLO enter. They walk around a little as others dance and make their way to the bar as the song ends.)*

JACK. Hey, everybody! Flash is here!

*(There are cheers and greetings from everyone in the Rabbit Hole. BARBARA and ROXY rush over to FLASH as SLY enters, unnoticed.)*

BARBARA. Hello, Flash! I'm Barbara Beaver, from First Forest News. I would like to interview you for our nightly sports report. This is my camera operator, Roxy Raccoon.

FLASH. Hi, Roxy. I haven't seen you since our race.

ROXY. *(bitter)* Do you still want to rub in how much you beat me?

FLASH. Aw, it wasn't that much, Rox.

TRIXIE. Yeah, only a mile or two.

*(TRIXIE and DIXIE giggle. BARBARA pulls FLASH forward as ROXY focuses the camera on them.)*

BARBARA. *(into camera)* Hello. I'm Barbara Beaver with First Forest News. With me is none other than Flash Hare, who will be racing Theodore Tortoise tomorrow morning. Flash, as I understand it, you will be named "Fastest Animal in the Forest" if you beat Theodore.

FLASH. You mean "when" I beat that tortoise.

BARBARA. My, you certainly sound sure of yourself. Don't you think that a tortoise might be able to beat a hare in a race?

*(FLASH, TRIXIE, DIXIE and some other animals that are listening begin to laugh.)*

FLASH. You're kidding, right?

BARBARA. Well, I guess it is a little improbable. Speaking of Theodore, where is he?

*(SLY steps forward.)*

SLY. He went home to rest before the race.

BARBARA. *(to FLASH)* Shouldn't you be doing the same? Resting and relaxing before the race, I mean.

FLASH. Are you kidding? Tonight is my Pre-Victory Party! I'll rest after the race, before my Victory Party. Come on, girls! Let's dance!

*(The music starts softly as FLASH leads TRIXIE, DIXIE and FLO onto the dance floor. They dance as BARBARA addresses the camera ROXY is holding.)*

BARBARA. *(to camera)* So, there you have it. Not only does Flash predict that he is going to win the race and become the fastest animal in the forest tomorrow, he is already celebrating his victory. Join us tomorrow morning at eight o'clock sharp for live coverage of the race. For First Forest News, I'm Barbara Beaver. Goodnight.

*(BARBARA and ROXY exit stage righ. The music rises as the animals dance. The curtains close and the lights dim.)*

## Scene Four

*(The lights are dim, indicating the wee hours of the morning.* **FLASH, TRIXIE, DIXIE** *and* **FLO** *enter stage left , stumbling. They are obviously exhausted.* **EDWINA OWL** *enters stage right.)*

**EDWINA.** Well, well, well. Look who it is. None other than the self-proclaimed "fastest animal in the forest."

**FLASH.** Hello, Edwina. Why are you up so late?

**EDWINA.** I'm an owl, Flash. It's what we do. You know…a nocturnal creature. We sleep during the day and go out at night.

**TRIXIE.** Then why aren't you out? Your nest is right up there.

*(***TRIXIE** *points up, off stage left.)*

**EDWINA.** The sun is going to come up any minute.

**DIXIE.** It is?

**EDWINA.** Yes. Don't you have a race to run today, Flash?

**FLASH.** No, it's tomorrow morning at eight o'clock.

**EDWINA.** Flash, it is tomorrow morning. Your race starts in less than three hours.

**FLASH.** Holy cabbage!

**FLO.** Why are you so upset, Flash? I thought you said you could beat Theo—

**FLASH.** *(interrupting)* I know what I said. I just have to go home and get ready for the race. I'll sleep when it's over. After I win, of course.

**TRIXIE.** *(yawning)* Okay, Flash. We'll see you at the starting line.

**EDWINA.** Good luck, Flash. It looks like you'll need it.

*(***EDWINA** *exits stage left as* **FLASH, TRIXIE, DIXIE** *and* **FLO** *exit stage right. The lights slowly come up until they are at full.)*

## Scene Five

*(Curtains open to reveal the start/finish line of the race. Almost all of the animals are milling around. They include **SLY**, **JACK**, **ROXY**, **BARBARA** and **THEODORE**, and any other animals that have been seen already except for **EDWINA**. **BARBARA** addresses the camera, held by **ROXY**.)*

**BARBARA.** Good morning! I'm Barbara Beaver from First Forest News, coming to you live from the center of the forest. In five minutes, the race to end all races will begin. Flash Hare has challenged Theodore Tortoise to a running race. If Flash wins, he will then be named the Fastest Animal in the Forest. With me now is the challenger, Theodore. Hello, Theo.

**THEODORE.** Hello, Barbara.

**BARBARA.** Do you mind if I ask you a couple of questions?

**THEODORE.** Not at all.

**BARBARA.** Do you really think that you can beat Flash?

**THEODORE.** You know what they say, Barbara. Slow and steady wins the race.

**BARBARA.** Tell me, Theo, how long have you been preparing for this race?

**THEODORE.** Well, I found out about it yesterday, so that makes it…

*(**THEODORE** begins counting on his fingers. As he does, **TRIXIE**, **DIXIE** and **FLO** hop in sluggishly, dressed as cheerleaders and carrying pompoms.)*

**BARBARA.** Oh! It looks like our champion has arrived!

*(**BARBARA**, **ROXY** and **THEODORE** clear the way for the bunnies. They are obviously exhausted and trudge through their cheer.)*

**TRIXIE, DIXIE & FLO.** *(wearily)*

Flash! Flash!

He's our hare!

If He can't do it…

*(TRIXIE, DIXIE and FLO all yawn.)*

FLO. I don't care.

*(FLASH enters, dragging his feet. All of the spectators cheer. TRIXIE, DIXIE and FLO huddle together at the edge of stage left and fall asleep.)*

FLASH. *(yawning)* Okay, everyone. Let's get this over with so I can go to sleep.

*(THEODORE and FLASH line up at the starting line.)*

THEO. Good luck, Flash.

FLASH. Yeah, yeah. You're a tortoise and I'm a hare. I don't need luck.

*(SLY stands in front of THEODORE and FLASH with his hands raised.)*

SLY. On your mark…

*(FLASH and THEODORE crouch into the starting position with their heads down.)*

SLY. Get set…

*(THEO looks up, but FLASH doesn't move.)*

SLY. GO!!!

*(SLY brings his hands down and gets out of the way. Everyone starts cheering. THEODORE slowly starts the race heading stage right. FLASH doesn't move. Everyone stops cheering abruptly. FLASH still hasn't moved. SLY walks over to FLASH.)*

SLY. Flash?

*(FLASH snores loudly.)*

SLY. Flash!

*(FLASH snorts and wakes up.)*

FLASH. Huh? What? Who? Huh?

SLY. I said "go."

FLASH. *(confused)* Go?

*(THEODORE is nearly off the stage by this point.)*

**THEODORE.** *(excited)* I'm winning! I'm winning!

**FLASH.** Oh! Go!

*(**FLASH** runs past **THEODORE**, down the stairs and into the audience. [NOTE: Great music for this section is The William Tell Overture.] **FLASH** runs up one aisle at top speed. **THEODORE** slowly follows. **FLASH** stops to rest at the last row in the audience and "falls asleep" near (or in the lap of) an audience member. **THEODORE** passes him. The audience will be shouting at **FLASH**. **FLASH** "wakes up" and runs past **THEODORE** again. Halfway down the aisle, he stops to rest and "falls asleep" for a second time. Again, **THEODORE** passes him. For the second time, **FLASH** "wakes up" and sprints past **THEODORE**. As **FLASH** runs onto the stage, the music fades. **FLASH** yawns and stretches.)*

**FLASH.** Boy, am I tired. The finish line is pretty close, and the bunnies will want to party as soon as I cross it. I need a quick nap.

*(**FLASH** looks into the audience and sees **THEODORE** slowly making his way to the stage.)*

**FLASH.** He's far enough behind for me to get forty winks and still beat him. I'll just stretch out right here.

*(**FLASH** leans against a tree and falls asleep. He snores loudly. **THEODORE** slowly makes his way onto the stage. He tiptoes past the sleeping **FLASH**, pauses, turns to the audience and makes the "shush" sign (finger to his lips), the continues toward the finish line. As he approaches the finish line, **SLY** motions to everyone to be quiet. **TRIXIE** stirs and wakes up. She turns and sees **THEODORE** nearing the finish line. She does a double take and jumps up.)*

**TRIXIE.** *(loudly)* Hey! Theo's beating Flash!

*(**DIXIE** and **FLO** wake up and jump to their feet.)*

**DIXIE.** Oh, no!

**FLO.** I knew it!

**TRIXIE.** *(calling to FLASH)* Flash! Flash! Wake up!

> *(The bunnies continue yelling to* **FLASH**. **FLASH** *wakes up.* **THEODORE** *is right in front of the finish line.* **FLASH** *runs across the stage just as* **THEODORE** *crosses the finish line. [NOTE: A very funny staging is to finish this scene in slow-motion with some slow music playing, such as the theme to* Chariots of Fire.* *Regular motion resumes as soon as* **THEODORE** *crosses the finish line.]* **THEODORE** *crosses the finish line and all of the animals cheer. There is a flurry of activity onstage.)*

**THEODORE.** I did it! I did it!

> *(***BARBARA** *runs over to* **THEODORE**, *followed by* **ROXY**.*)*

**BARBARA.** *(to camera)* This is Barbara Beaver reporting live from the finish line. We have just witnessed the upset of the century! Theodore Tortoise has just beaten Flash Hare in a running race. Theo, now that you have won the title of Fastest Animal in the Forest, what are you going to do?

**THEODORE.** I'm going to Dis—

> *(***TRIXIE**, **DIXIE** *and* **FLO** *run to center stage. Their cheer interrupts* **THEODORE**. *During the cheer,* **TRIXIE**, **DIXIE** *and* **FLO** *encourage the audience to participate.)*

**TRIXIE, DIXIE & FLO.** Give us a T!

**ANIMALS.** T!

**TRIXIE, DIXIE & FLO.** Give us an H!

**ANIMALS.** H!

**TRIXIE, DIXIE & FLO.** Give us an E!

**ANIMALS.** E!

**TRIXIE, DIXIE & FLO.** Give us an O!

**ANIMALS.** O!

**TRIXIE, DIXIE & FLO.** What does that spell?

**ANIMALS.** Theo!

---

*Please see Music Use Note on Page 3.

*(Again, all of the animals cheer.* JACK *shouts above the noise.)*

JACK. Come on, everybody! Let's go to the Rabbit Hole! Carrot juice is on the house!

*(All of the animals cheer again.* THEODORE *is lifted up and carried out like a hero. They exit stage left.* FLASH *is left staring after them.* SLY *stands upstage from* FLASH.*)*

SLY. So—

FLASH. *(interrupting)* Don't say it.

SLY. Don't say what?

FLASH. You told me so. I know, I know.

SLY. I didn't tell you anything.

FLASH. Sure you did. You said that I couldn't call myself the fastest animal in the forest until I beat Theodore. *(a beat)* How did you know that I was going to lose?

SLY. I didn't know you were going to lose, Flash. I just had a hunch. You were too sure of yourself, Flash, so you made a lot of mistakes. You didn't believe that Theo could actually beat you, so you didn't try your best.

FLASH. I guess I should always try my best.

SLY. Yes, you should. Theo won because he was prepared. He concentrated and focused on the race. Like I told Theo—

FLASH. *(interrupting)* I know, I know. Slow and steady wins the race. I'll be more prepared next time.

SLY. Good. Now, let's get to the Rabbit Hole. I believe you have a hat to eat.

*(FLASH *thinks a moment, then remembers.)*

FLASH. Oh, no! Flo's hat!

*(SLY *starts leading* FLASH *off stage left.)*

SLY. Don't worry. I'm sure you can wash it down with some carrot juice.

*(SLY *and* FLASH *exit stage left as the curtains close.)*

**THE END**

**Also by**
**Candice Cain...**

# The Woodsmen and
# The Fairy

# OTHER TITLES AVAILABLE FROM BAKER'S PLAYS

## THE WOODSMEN AND THE FAIRY

### Candice Cain

*Children's Theatre, TYA / 2m, 1f*

Henry is a simple and happy woodsman. Every day, he chops trees down and sells them at the market. One day, his friend Jim startles him and Henry drops his axe into a pond. Lily, the water fairy of the pond, appears and retrieves Henry's axe. She gives Henry a test to find out his honesty, and Henry passes with flying colors. As a reward for telling the truth, Lily gives Henry two ornate axes. Jim finds out about Henry's good fortune, and seeks Lily for his own gain. He drops his axe in the same pond, and Lily appears. Lily gives Jim the same test to find out how honest he is, and Jim fails miserably. To punish him for lying, Lily turns Jim into a tree. Jim finally learns the importance of telling the truth and being honest, and becomes a man once again.

Based on one of Aesop's fables, *The Woodsman and the Fairy* teaches children the importance of being honest and telling the truth. *The Woodsman and the Fairy* is a brief, yet fun and educational play for children ages 5 – 9. There is a great deal of audience participation in this play, which keeps the audience involved and interested. Only three actors are required for this play: Jim, Lily, and Henry. The entire story takes place in one area of the woods. During one scene, the action takes place in front of the curtains. The costumes are simple. Because of the minimal production requirements, this makes an excellent play for any group to perform, either formally or informally.

# OTHER TITLES AVAILABLE FROM BAKER'S PLAYS

## THREEE: THREE FUNNY FOLKTALES

### Colleen Neuman

*Folktales / Flexible casts of 9 to 31 / Simple sets*

Three very funny folktales from the author of our immensely popular *Princess Plays* and *Lion and Mouse Stories.*

**The Lion Who Roared**
*Flexible cast of 20-31 or more / very simple set, costumes and props*
Lion's roaring is keeping the other animals in the jungle awake night after night. Zebra, Elephant, Leopard, Antelope and Hyena go to Lion and nervously request that he roar quietly. When Lion roars his refusal, Zebra announces that there is a new animal in the jungle that is bigger, stronger, louder than Lion. Lion, furious, challenges this Popalopalus to three contests to prove who is mightiest. Zebra runs home and confesses he made it up. There is no Popalopalus. So they use all the jungle animals to build one. Ostrich, Python, Rhinoceros and Gazelle are the legs, Giraffe is the head, Mrs. Armadillo and her children are the tail and so on. When this creature wins all three contests, Lion stops roaring and starts whispering.

**A Fair Price**
*Flexible cast of 9-17 or more / very simple set, costumes and props*
Three women are about to be cheated. A cart driver is demanding that a woman pay him three copper coins for sitting in the shadow of his cart. A baker demands another woman pay three copper coins for smelling his honey cakes. A peddler requires a third woman to pay three copper coins when she overhears the music of a flute he demonstrates for a customer. All three women refuse to pay and take their cases to a wise woman who tells them they must pay a fair price. The first woman is told to pay the cart driver with the shadows of three copper coins. The second woman pays the baker with the smell of three copper coins. The third woman shakes three copper coins and pays the peddler with the sound of them rattling.

**Banana Sandwich In A Boat**
*Flexible cast of 15-22 or more / very simple set, costumes and props*
A man and woman are about to be married when the groom announces that their firstborn child will be named Banana Sandwich In A Boat. The bride's father denounces him as a fool and calls off the wedding. The groom proposes that if he can find three people more foolish than himself the wedding will go on. The father agrees. First the groom finds a man so foolish that in order to put on his pants he climbs a tree, aims for the pants on the ground and jumps. Next he meets a woman who has built a house with no windows and is dumping buckets of sunshine into the house in order to get some light. Last, he finds a crowd arguing over how to get a woman riding a donkey into their village because the woman keeps banging her head on the archway over the gate. Half of them want to chop off the woman's head and the other half want to chop off the donkey's legs. The father sees that the groom is not nearly so foolish as the rest of the world and gives his blessing to the newlyweds.

# AESOP'S (OH SO SLIGHTLY) UPDATED FABLES

## Kim Esop-Wylie

*Comedy / 30+ gender-flexible parts, doubling & tripling / May be done with as few as 8 actors*

This short play, performed for and with kids, weaves five of Aesop's most famous fables into a show that's fun, fast-paced, and full of surprises.

Contains: The Dog and the Bone; The Tortoise and the Hare; The Lion and the Mouse; The Fox and the Grapes; The Miller, His Son And the Donkey, and The Country Maid.

From the author of *The Dullsville Mystery*

# THE ANGRY EAGLE FEATHER

## Julie Tosh

*Modern Fable / 6m, 4f, possible doubling and extras / Unit Set*

From the author of *Beauty of the Century* and *Pharaoh's Revenge* comes a beautiful modem Native American fable with a universal message. Ruth MacAfferty has a problem. First of all, for a third grader she gets too much homework. She also has a disinterested older brother Jacob and a know-it-all older sister Sarah. But life as she knows it comes to a crashing halt when a golden eagle feather falls from the sky to land at her feet. Her first mistake is picking it up. Her second is telling anyone she has it. Because now Ruth is a criminal. She is breaking the law of the United States by possessing a protected religious symbol of Native American tribes everywhere. On top of that, the feather has started talking to her, and it isn't happy sitting in her backpack day after day. Jacob thinks she should see someone in government. Sarah thinks she should take it back to where she got it. But, when Ruth's teacher suggests she get help at the nearby reservation. Ruth and her angry eagle feather both find a spiritual home.

Breinigsville, PA USA
10 December 2010
251126BV00005B/1/P

9 780874 407396